The Shipwreck

With fairy best wishes
Hayley x

S 2021

Also by Hayley Dartnell

Lavender Fairy Adventures Series:
Book 1: *The Escape*

Adult fiction:
The Windfall
(published as part of the best-selling
Connections collection)

Lavender Fairy
Adventures

The Shipwreck

Hayley Dartnell

Illustrated by Stella Mirabella

First published by Fuzzy Flamingo 2021
© 2021 Hayley Dartnell

© 2021 Illustrations by StellaMirabella
www.stellamirabella.de

Paperback ISBN: 978-1-8384388-6-9

A CIP catalogue record for this book is available from the
British Library

Cover design and typesetting: Fuzzy Flamingo
www.fuzzyflamingo.co.uk

In loving memory of Ronald James Walter
1939 – 2020

Prologue

"Go!" encouraged Lyra in a low voice. "And stay safe all of you."

With a flap of their wings, the blackbirds set off. The rain had eased but danger was still lurking. A rustle in the bushes indicated they were not alone. Milly the mouse slipped quietly away into the shadows as Lyra and Apple turned to face Blackskull the Moth.

"Did George escape?" the head of the Marsh Beast Gang asked quietly, keeping his voice to a murmur.

Both fairies nodded as Blackskull thanked them.

"But you must leave immediately," the moth added. "Remember the curse? Dark Arches is still out there. Go, before he sees you both," he whispered urgently just as a cry from the darkness rang out.

"This isn't the end!" Dark Arches cried from the shadows. "We will be back to have our revenge on you all, then you'll be sorry!"

The moth's final words echoed into the night sky.

Chapter 1

The Blackbird Sisters, Bibi and Bow, took flight from the garden of Crumble Cottage. Making sure that George the Moth was tucked securely under Bibi's wing, they left Bluebell Meadow behind and soared into the sky. They travelled at speed through the darkness until the weather took a turn for the worse, hindering their journey with fierce winds and heavy showers, sending them off course and into unchartered territory.

Now desperately seeking shelter to avoid the rainfall, Bibi and Bow flew unknowingly into the depths of a haunted forest. Clusters of ancient trees sensed strangers in their midst and began shaking their dark silvery leaves excitedly in anticipation, stretching out their gnarly long

Hayley Dartnell

branches resembling arms, hands and fingers, hoping to snatch the birds that were heading their way.

But the Blackbird Sisters were nimble. They swooped high then low, cleverly swerving the clumsy grasps of the trees. They fled without capture but ended up in a deeper and much darker part of the forest, discovering an abandoned nest. The shabby dwelling made of dried twigs and a few matted feathers provided the trio with the briefest of respites. Just a moment later, a high-pitched scream ripped through the entire forest, then silence fell.

When an owl hooted loudly, and a group of bats made a sudden departure, Bibi and Bow felt very nervous. From the safety of Bibi's wing, George could feel her tension. But desperate for a glimpse of the outside world, he gently lifted a dark brown feather. He quickly retracted when he caught sight of a headless horseman charging through the glen on a dark grey stallion. The sound of horse's hooves galloping straight towards them frightened the trio. They wasted no more time and were airborne within seconds. Their destination was the Norfolk coast and they were determined to reach it.

Chapter 2

George and the Blackbird Sisters finally arrived in the quiet Norfolk seaside village of Old Honeystone. The blue hour had passed, and dawn was breaking, so they took refuge on the ruins of St Edmund's Chapel. An archway, constructed mainly of carrstone and flintstone rubble, was all that remained of the former parish church. It had been built in medieval times and now sat just metres away from the clifftop edge in a World War One memorial garden.

Bow, the elder of the blackbirds, waited a few moments until George had carefully extracted himself from the confines of Bibi's wing before asking her a question.

"What do you think of your new home,

George?" she said, nodding her head towards the magnificent lighthouse that stood before them.

George took a shaky step forward, nearly slipping on an exposed piece of flint. Feeling completely overwhelmed, he gazed in wonder at the tall white structure. Its origins dated back to eighteen hundred and forty, designed to guide vessels safely into the deep waters of the bay. The disused lighthouse stood proudly in the former Victorian resort, with a perfect view out to sea, also known as The Wash.

Their journey overall had been quite the ordeal, so the blackbirds respected George's continued silence and made themselves comfortable on a piece of moss. They were just closing their eyes to rest when out of nowhere a cold white mist suddenly appeared. It crept up the side of the ancient stones and curled itself tightly around George and the sisters.

George felt his anxiety levels rise as the mist tried desperately hard to lift them off their feet. And just when he thought it would succeed, a sudden cry pierced the air loudly from a lone seagull circling overhead. The mist reluctantly unfurled itself with a tinkle of laughter and disappeared into the long grasses below. Shaken,

Bibi, Bow and George nodded gratefully to the seagull as it hovered in the early morning sky.

"The White Mist likes to scare newcomers but means no harm," explained the gull, looking directly at George. "Welcome to Old Honeystone, my friends, I'll see you again very soon!" Then with a flap of his large, majestic white wings, the giant bird flew out to sea.

As the sun began to rise, it suddenly became clear to Bow, the elder blackbird sister, that this area of Norfolk was a hive of mystery and magic. Bibi was thinking exactly the same thought and suggested to George that now would be a good time to check out the lighthouse. So together they flew across the grassy verge to a melody sung by nearby songbirds who were jovially signalling daybreak.

Chapter 3

As the summer months rolled by, George was thoroughly enjoying his new life in Old Honeystone. His new home at the top of the beautiful lighthouse was spacious and homely, thanks to the help of his neighbours Scruffy and Flash, a pair of elderly robins who lived in the downstairs hedgerow. The surrounding areas were a delight to explore, and he'd even made a few new friends. Dave the seagull was one of them, and a mermaid called Savannah.

On calm, sunny days, George would sit for hours with Savannah on the rocks that carpeted the shoreline below the clifftop. He loved listening to her historical tales of tall ships, ghosts and smugglers. By night, her

dulcet tones filled the twilight air as she sang enchanting little lullabies that sent him off to a peaceful sleep.

On the stormiest of days, George would recall the night he and the Blackbird Sisters had made their escape from Bluebell Meadow. He had run away from a notorious gang of moths, known as the Marsh Beasts, who lived there too. George had been part of the group for such a long time until one day he had felt brave enough to leave. But his sudden departure had led him into danger and he sustained an injury, but managed to fly to safety and send out an SOS. The call for help had arrived in the form of a Lavender Fairy called Apple, aptly named after a piece of fruit. Whilst Apple set about repairing George's broken wing, he spoke of his dream of living by the sea. So, with the help of the Lavender Fairies, a plan was devised to smuggle George safely out of Bluebell Meadow. And the mission had worked. But George missed Apple terribly. She had become a very good friend in a short space of time and a great influence on his life. But he was happy, and his confidence was growing more each day, filled with real friends, and it was all thanks to Apple.

Chapter 4

One particularly stormy evening in October, George was sitting at home in his favourite spot, the porthole, a tiny round window at the top of the lighthouse. A makeshift ledge, fashioned from a small piece of driftwood, provided the perfect viewpoint across the bay. There would be no sunset tonight as the moody dark grey skies had obscured it from vision, but George didn't mind. He was happy enough to watch the waves crash back and forth over the rocks below the cliff and the inbound tide claw relentlessly at the pebbles. A repetitive, but also useless, game of trying to lure the tiny stones into the sea. The salty water was always unsuccessful but left its mark anyway by temporarily leaving trails of foamy white bubbles in its wake.

As the sky grew darker, George caught the reflection of his beautiful silver wings, tinged with purple, glowing in the single pane of glass. They looked exactly the same as Apple's wings on the day they had met. Bright and sparkly, he thought, smiling fondly at the memory. This was quite a revelation for George because he'd always been very forgetful. But that had all changed when he met Apple the Lavender Fairy and now he could remember all sorts of things.

Confused by this sudden influx of memories, he asked the Blackbird Sisters for their advice during their brief stay at the lighthouse. Bibi and Bow had answered happily.

"When Apple the Lavender Fairy repaired your wing, the potion she used contained two very important ingredients. Magic and lavender," explained Bibi.

"The lavender has a natural healing property and it therefore restored your memory. And the magic came directly from the Lavender Fairy herself," said Bow.

"And when the time is right, George, your newly manifested powers will be of assistance to others." The blackbirds pointed to a familiar looking item on the opposite side of the attic. A gazing ball, sitting on an old wooden barrel. A communication tool that all the Lavender Fairies used. George thought it looked like a coloured glass marble filled with tiny air bubbles. It was nestled in a soft bed of moss, mounted on a thin slice of wood to stop it from rolling away. George remembered clearly how Apple had used her own device to contact Lyra, Queen of the Lavender Fairies. Apple had simply tapped twice on the glass and said Lyra's name out loud. Moments later, Lyra appeared inside the ball and both fairies could see, hear and talk to each other.

As day turned to night, George glanced over at the gazing ball, wondering if he'd ever need to use it, when it suddenly lit up and illuminated the room. George's eyes grew wide with shock. It had been dormant for all these months, why choose to light up now? Perhaps it was Apple calling to say hello, thought George hopefully, fluttering over to it expecting to see the Lavender Fairy inside.

But what he saw was someone completely different!

Chapter 5

A young boy, aged around eight or nine, was inside the gazing ball waving his hands with excitement. His cheeky little smile, bright blue eyes and tousled wet hair warmed George's heart immediately.

George pressed himself up closer to the glass. By way of hello, he fluttered his silvery wings, now glowing brightly in the darkness.

"You can see me!?" exclaimed the boy.

"Yes I can!" replied George, feeling extremely confused having never spoken to a human being before, but remembering his manners. "I'm George," he said, hoping he sounded friendly. "What's your name?"

"Hello, George, I'm Tom," he said with a smile. "I'm on the beach," Tom continued

excitedly "Do you want to come and play in the rock pools?"

The beach? At this time of night, and all alone? George tore himself away from the gazing ball and flew back to the window. The tide was high, and the full moon was trying to squeeze past the storm clouds to cast her full beam of light across the bay. And, just for a few seconds, she managed it, just as the waves had built up their momentum and were thrashing themselves over the rocks.

George scanned the beach as far as he could, but there was no sign of the young boy. When a sudden chill filled the room, the light in the glass ball went out. George's wings began to tingle, and he knew instinctively that the connection had been lost.

Chapter 6

The very next day, George was up early replaying the events that had happened the night before. Had he dreamt the whole thing? Had the gazing ball really lit up all by itself? And had he really spoken to a human being?

George couldn't explain any of it but was certainly very curious. At daybreak, and with the tide out, he decided to fly down to the beach and take a look. Taking his usual route, he followed the stripy coloured cliffs down towards the sandy shoreline and discovered the skeletal remains of a boat. It lay in a watery grave surrounded by golden coloured sand, covered in barnacles and draped with seaweed. The salty water had left behind various sized

rock pools too. George settled on a large piece of rock and watched as a family of tiny crabs scuttled by quickly and buried themselves in the sand. George scoured the beach, but there was no sign of Tom. Just a handful of tourists taking photos of the shipwreck.

This is all very odd, thought George, taking one final look around for the young boy. When suddenly he had a lightbulb moment. He knew exactly who could help. Savannah! The mermaid had never mentioned the lonely shipwreck but perhaps would know of its origins. Knowing where to find her, George immediately took flight in the direction of the rocks, situated directly beneath the lighthouse. With excitement surging through his glittery wings, George found the beautiful mermaid sitting in her favourite place. She was basking in the sunlight, combing her long blonde hair with her fishtail submerged in a deep pool of water. As George approached, Savannah was careful not to splash her friend with delight.

However as predicted, Savannah was a font of all knowledge. She confirmed that the shipwreck on the beach was a former steam trawler. It had been painted bright yellow during World War Two and used as a patrol vessel.

On the night of a terrible storm in April 1947, the boat had broken free from its moorings in the market town of Kings Lynn. A fierce wind had driven the unmanned boat across the bay, also known as The Wash. It is a rectangular-shaped bay and estuary in the north-west corner of East Anglia on the east coast of England. It's where Norfolk meets Lincolnshire and both counties border the North Sea. Sadly, the steam trawler met its untimely demise when it hit the rocks at Honeystone Beach.

"All that remains today is the rusty metal ribcage," explained Savannah, all matter of fact.

"But what happened to the boy?" George asked, hoping there would be some information about the young lad. Puzzlement automatically clouded the beautiful mermaid's face.

"What boy?" asked Savannah.

Now it was George's turn to explain.

Chapter 7

Later that night, George sat in the porthole looking out across The Wash. The tragic story of the former steam trawler playing over in his head.

"But what is the connection to the boy?" George said out loud, sighing with frustration. He fluttered over to the barrel where the magical glass ball sat, willing it to light up.

An hour passed by, and George's request was answered. As the globe lit up, George smiled with delight.

"Hello George!" yelled Tom excitedly. "Please can you help me?"

But before George could answer, the connection was lost yet again.

"Tom, come back!" cried George. "Tom, if

you can hear me, please come back." But as the minutes ticked by, there was still no response. George began fluttering madly around the attic, frustrated with not being able to help. But he knew someone who could. The Lavender Fairies!

Chapter 8

George recalled the simple instructions and gently tapped the glass ball and called out Lyra's name. The Queen of the Lavender Fairies appeared a few moments later with Apple by her side. Within half an hour, the three friends had a plan of action. And a few days later, Gypsy the Psychic Fairy arrived at the lighthouse. George liked her immediately. The bohemian fairy stood in the doorway to the attic room carrying a very large orange handbag made from wool. At her feet lay a wicker basket filled with goodies covered with a red and white chequered cloth. And by her side was a small wooden broomstick with its handle entwined with brightly coloured ribbons.

"Hello, George, I'm Gypsy," she exclaimed,

walking directly into George's home. Her dark eyes lit up at the sight of the gazing ball as she pegged up her cloak on an old nail jutting out of the wall. She took off her tiny little orange hat that matched her bag and shook out her hair, setting aside her broomstick and quickly making herself at home.

A stunned George just sat in silence. Mesmerised by her personality and organisation skills, he watched as she began to empty the contents of her brightly coloured bag.

"Help yourself to the flowers from the basket, George, whilst I make some tea," Gypsy said, unpacking a small teacup fashioned from an acorn and adding a handful of fresh nettles. Smiling cheerily, she poured cold water from a flask made from a walnut and onto the leaves. She snapped her fingers and the water in the cup began to steam. George watched on in utter amazement at such magic as he clutched the stem of a daisy. Her long black curly pigtails bounced wildly around her beautiful face as she spread a handmade patchwork blanket across the bare floor. She then plumped up several large cushions to make a comfortable seating area. Lifting the cloth from the basket, she produced a slice of chocolate cake from a box. Popping it

on a small china plate, she snapped her fingers once more at a lone cork, turning it instantly into a side table. Then with a contented sigh, the busy fairy plopped herself onto a cushion and reached for her cup of tea.

"Now then, George," Gypsy said, flicking a pigtail out of the way and taking a sip of her hot drink. "Start from the beginning and do not miss a single thing out."

Chapter 9

George and Gypsy waited patiently all evening for the gazing ball to light up, but they were sadly disappointed. The fairy could see that George was desperate to help the young boy, so they made plans to visit the shipwreck the very next day. The information from Savannah the mermaid had provided them with some insight towards the wreckage, but none about the small child.

Exhausted from her journey, Gypsy suggested they both get a good night's sleep and start afresh in the morning. George agreed and helped to pull out blankets from the magical orange bag. Together they made up a lovely huge bed, mostly to accommodate Gypsy's wild black pigtails. Minutes later, the tired pair were fast asleep and missed the gazing ball flicker.

Chapter 10

The following day, the tide had revealed its underwater kingdom on the beach. George and Gypsy sat side by side on one of the metal spines of the shipwreck's rusty ribcage. Surrounding the wreckage were dozens of rock pools and huge slate-grey boulders, peppering the beach like giant stepping stones and glistening with moisture in the early morning sunshine. There was not a human being in sight and the only sounds were of the cries from hungry seagulls circling above in the cool autumn sky. One of them was Dave, George's friend. Having spotted the duo, he had waved 'hello' then flown off with speed in search of food in the direction of Holme-next-the-Sea, a local nature reserve.

Gypsy sniffed the fresh sea air. The saltiness lifted her senses, rejuvenated her mind and also reminded her that Halloween was fast approaching. It was her most favourite time of the year when the veil of the two worlds were at its thinnest. This gave Gypsy an idea and she fluttered down to the edge of the deepest rock pool within the hull of the shipwreck.

"I wonder…?" Gypsy began to say, as she gathered her long dark curls together, knotting them with a scarf she produced from inside her cloak pocket, preventing them from dangling in the water. George sensed that he should not interrupt her. He just watched instead with fascination as her gossamer wings sparkled naturally in the sunlight, brushing her fingertips over the water in a swirly motion. His eyes bulged with amazement when a little boy's face slowly appeared. The fairy's magic was working!

"Hello, Tom," said Gypsy with a warm smile. "Our friend George here has been looking for you."

The little boy grinned and clapped his hands with joy.

Chapter 11

Tom's Story, June 1938 - April 1947

I t was a beautiful spring day in Norfolk when Tom ran away from Marchborough Hall. It was a grand stately home surrounded by countryside that had been converted into an orphanage at the beginning of the Second World War. The owners, Lord and Lady March, had offered their home to the government. It was part of the war effort to house the children being evacuated from London who were referred to as 'Evacuees'. Many of them had already lost their families to the casualties of war-torn Britain and were transported to available homes all around the country for safety.

Marchborough Hall was part of a country

estate that could accommodate lots of children, Tom being one of them. The exterior of the building was very imposing with steps leading up to a portico, housing a grand front door. Equally stunning were the grounds and fields beyond. But, behind the façade, that was where the beauty ended. Inside the house, dozens of rooms were filled with priceless antique furniture, all covered in ghostly white dustsheets. Long chilly corridors were devoid of rugs and console tables and dirty grey shadows marked the walls where family portraits once hung. Extensive parquet flooring throughout the downstairs required constant sweeping and there were too many windows to count that needed washing on a regular basis. It was also miles from the nearest town, the market town of Kings Lynn.

Tom had lost his entire family when he was only four years old. Their home, a small terraced house in London's East End, had been one of the many casualties of World War Two. A doodlebug had exploded and demolished the entire street where they lived. Tom, the only survivor, had been found barely alive beneath the rubble by a team of volunteers. He'd then been taken to the London Hospital on Whitechapel Road for treatment and had woken up three weeks later.

"Where is my family?" Tom had asked when he had regained consciousness, remembering clearly the blast that had hit their home.

"They are all in heaven, my dear," a kind young nurse had very quietly and gently explained. "You will see them again one day," she continued, as Tom wept with grief in her arms.

With no other family to take care of him, Tom was discharged from hospital and evacuated to Norfolk. He and lots of other children had boarded a train at London Fields Station and were then transported by coach to a village hall just outside of Thetford. They were all escorted inside to the waiting area where the local women were gathered. Many scrutinised Tom's second-hand clothes, grubby little face and the gas mask tin that was slung over his shoulder and simply walked on by. As the hall began to empty, Tom was left standing on his own and beginning to feel that nobody wanted him. He was on the verge of tears when an elderly couple entered the room. Tom's heart filled with hope at the sight of them and hurriedly brushed his watery eyes with the back of his sleeve and grinned with all his might.

"Are we too late?" they asked the stern-looking woman who was in charge of the billeting.

"There is only one child left," came the curt reply from the tired young woman who sat at her desk surrounded by paperwork.

The kind old lady and her husband glanced across the room at Tom, their eyes lighting up in pure delight, and immediately asked Tom if he would like to come and live with them.

He spent the next four happy years with Mrs M and Pops, as he liked to call them, until the day they died. Mrs M suffered two heart attacks. The first was a warning and the second one was fatal. Unable to live without his wife, Pops died shortly after of a broken heart. Tom was devastated. In less than three weeks he had lost the closest two people he had to family and, aged only eight years old, was homeless again. The local child authorities had stepped in, and Tom was immediately taken into temporary care. Two days later, on a very cold, wet and windy day in November, he arrived at Marchborough Hall.

Chapter 12

Tom's Story 1946 - 1947

Tom had been living at the orphanage for six long miserable months. Not a day went by without thinking of his beloved Pops and Mrs M and he missed them desperately. The other children in the home were friendly enough, and in similar circumstances, but it wasn't the same. Night after night he could hear the muffled sobs of the younger ones crying into their pillows for their mothers. Tom would brush away his silent tears, not wanting to be the subject of ridicule by the other boys the next day for sporting puffy eyes. The very strict matron, who was in charge and extremely unkind, would also notice. Punishment for

crying would be a day, sometimes two, in the cellar without food and water. It was a foul-smelling room located beneath the ground level of Marchborough Hall, built entirely from stone and used for storing vegetables during the winter months. The damp, dark, windowless basement was a scary place to be for a child of any age. The low bearing ceiling had no natural light, was covered with cobwebs and housed large black hairy spiders. A family of mice lived down there too, and you could hear their tiny claws scuttle over the cold cobbled stone floor. The only way in, and out, was via a steep narrow staircase behind a heavy wooden door located in the pantry. Matron would march a child at speed towards the cellar door, making them walk down the cold steps alone and into darkness. She would then close the door with a bang and return to collect them at bedtime. But her cruelty didn't end there. 'Her Royal Meanness' as Tom liked to call her, made all the children do countless chores. It was her way of keeping them disciplined and the stately home clean and tidy.

One of Tom's weekly tasks was to clean the parquet flooring in the grand entrance hall. It was backbreaking work, as he would be on his hands and knees all morning with a large brush, scrubbing the busy walkway. During this time, he would have traipsed back and forth to the pantry to refill his bucket with clean soapy water. By midday, Tom would be absolutely ravenous. When he lived with Pops and Mrs M, she would serve a delicious hot meal every day at twelve o'clock. It would include a large portion of meat, potatoes, a selection of tasty vegetables and a huge jug of homemade gravy. Meals at the orphanage were a stark comparison. Under Matron's strict instructions, Cook would ladle warm watery vegetable broth into very small bowls at lunchtime. The tasteless soup was served with a thin slice of stale bread without any butter or dripping. Tom would quickly finish his meal, as he was always hungry, and block out the memory of the proper homemade food he used to love.

On a particularly sunny April morning, Tom was about to refill his bucket when he spotted a freshly baked loaf of bread. It was resting on a wooden chopping board alongside a jar of strawberry jam and a pat of butter in the pantry. Placing his empty bucket on the quarry tiled floor, his stomach immediately grumbled loudly with hunger. Then, without thinking,

he grabbed it, tearing off a huge chunk and savouring the taste. Breaking off the opposite end of the bread, he was just about to dip the crust into the enticingly good preserve when he heard familiar footsteps. They belonged to Matron. He hadn't heard her approach until it was too late. Freezing with fear, Tom turned around slowly to face her.

"How dare you steal from me!" roared Matron, glaring at Tom ferociously. Her high-pitched voice reached as many decibels as humanly possible and enough to make his ears ring with pain. Her anger extended to the heavy basket of vegetables she'd been carrying, and she slammed it down with force onto the table. It toppled over immediately, spilling the contents all over the floor. Matron reached towards him with both arms poised in the air, hands forming a crab-like grasp. But Tom knew what was coming. Matron would surely lock him up in the cellar for at least a week as punishment for stealing the bread. Perhaps longer. But never again, thought Tom, as he gazed up at her ugly face one last time. Never again would he be treated so cruelly by the hands of this woman. He snatched up the loaf, tucking it under his arm, and ducked underneath the large kitchen table. Scrambling quickly across the pantry floor, he dodged the loose potatoes, turnips and beetroot that were rolling towards him. He ran quickly out of the side door and into the garden, resisting the urge to grab a loose turnip and fling it at the horrible woman.

The resident gardener, who was busy mowing the lawn, had heard Matron shouting. Raising his thick bushy eyebrows with surprise, he watched the young boy race straight past him and disappear through a small gap in a hedge.

"Come back here this instant you little thief!" screamed Matron, running after Tom, waving her fists tightly in the air.

"You won't catch that young fellow," muttered the gardener to himself, knowing full well not to antagonise the angry woman. "He's gone!"

Chapter 13

Tom ran until nightfall and found an empty tree trunk to shelter in. Curling up inside, the sound of heavy raindrops hitting the ground soon lulled him into a deep sleep. He awoke late the next morning clutching the half-eaten loaf of bread. It was a bit stale but still edible and would provide some energy until his next meal at least. With no idea of where he was or where he was going, Tom just started walking. Hours later he found himself in Kings Lynn, a large seaport and market town with a harbour. Catching sight of a bright yellow steam trawler moored at the docks, he went over to admire the magnificent vessel.

Tom loved big ships and wanted to be a sailor when he grew up. He and Pops had

often talked about it, but Mrs M was dead set against his grand plans to sail the seven seas. Curiosity got the better of him and he wandered up the gang plank. Stepping onboard the stream trawler, Tom gazed around in wonder at the huge wooden crates stacked around him. Wondering what was in them, he took a peek inside one that was open, just as a large rat was scuttling past. Tom let out a ticklish squeal as its long tail brushed against his bare ankle.

"Jim, is that you?" a man's gruff voice called out loudly.

Startled, Tom looked around for somewhere to hide when he heard the man's heavy footsteps coming towards him. Quickly ducking down a narrow flight of steps, he hid underneath a pile of empty hessian sacks and held his breath. A moment later, Tom heard the footsteps march across the deck above and a loud bang indicated something was being closed shut. Sighing with relief, Tom climbed out from the mass of brown scratchy material and noticed a pile of sandbags in a corner. Exhausted from his escape from the orphanage and the hours of walking, he crawled gratefully onto the makeshift bed. He had felt brave running away from the awful Matron. But where was he going to live now? Seconds later, the gentle movement of the ship made the young boy close his eyes and drift off to sleep.

Chapter 14

Many hours later, Tom awoke with a start and couldn't remember where he was. He slowly rubbed his eyes, hoping that would help as he stared into the darkness. His memory was jolted within an instant. Realising he'd fallen asleep onboard the huge vessel, it was now moving somewhat erratically and making the most awful noise.

"Hello?!" Tom cried out in panic. "Hello! Can anyone hear me?" But his plea went unheard as the trawler had no crew. Swinging his legs off the makeshift bed, Tom unknowingly plunged his bare feet into freezing cold water. He gasped in shock when the water reached his knees and quickly scrambled back onto the safety of the sandbags.

Under attack from the elements, the sea trawler howled in pain. The fierce wind and rain brutally thrashed against its unmanned walls, whistling harshly as it tore through its heart. Tom could hear the wooden crates above filled with cargo crash and slide with every movement of the boat's frenzy. They were in the eye of the storm and the huge angry waves were driving the sea trawler further towards the rocks at Honeystone Beach. The air tasted heavily of salt as gallons more water gushed inside, quickly filling the confines of the lower decks as it was hurled across The Wash.

Scared for his life, Tom remembered the narrow staircase he had descended earlier that day, but it would mean jumping into the water and wading across. But before he could take another step forward, the boat cried out once more in terror. Terrified, Tom reached for a nearby handrail. He clung tightly for support, unable to block his ears with his hands to shut out the deafening noise. Then, as the trawler shuddered to an ear-piercing halt, sea water flooded every inch of available space, claiming the territory for itself, leaving poor Tom with no hope of escape.

Chapter 15

As Tom finished his story, George wiped away a tear. He hadn't realised he had been talking to a ghost.

"Please can you help me find my family?" Tom asked hopefully.

Despite just having relived his ordeal, he smiled as he rose out of the rock pool to stand before George and Gypsy on the beach. George wanted nothing more than to help young Tom find his long-lost family after being trapped onboard a shipwreck since that fateful night.

But how? thought George to himself, his antenna poised in a thoughtful position, turning towards Gypsy. She answered him telepathically, taking him by surprise.

"Have faith, George," she said, turning her

attention back to the matter at hand.

"Thank you, Tom, for sharing your story with us," Gypsy said out loud, her voice full of warmth and kindness.

"Of course we can help you!"

Gypsy then whispered some very special words and waited. Moments later, a small figure could be seen walking towards them from a distance. Tom stood very still, squinting his eyes at the image on the deserted beach.

"Is that my mum?" Tom asked hesitantly, as the person became more visible.

"Yes, Tom, it is," confirmed Gypsy softly. "She has been searching for you for a very long time. Go and say hello."

George's eyes bulged with bewilderment as he watched the young boy jump off a rock and race to greet his mother.

"Gypsy, how did you make that happen?" George exclaimed in awe. She just smiled and gave a little wink. They watched Tom run at speed straight towards his mother's open arms. She bent down and scooped up her long-lost child into a huge embrace. Swinging him around and covering his head with kisses, she laughed with joy.

"Thank you, George and Gypsy!" mother

and son chorused, as they stood side by side on the beach holding hands. They slowly turned to face a beam of brilliant white light that had suddenly appeared. It dimmed to a very soft warm glow, revealing three more people. Tom's father and his two younger sisters. Reunited at last, the whole family turned to wave their final goodbyes and stepped into the light together.

Chapter 16

Back at the lighthouse, George was sitting in his favourite spot watching Gypsy pack her last few items. He was feeling a little sad that his newest friend was leaving, but then the gazing ball lit up.

"And where do you think you're going?" shouted a well-spoken woman. "I need both of you for this job!"

Excitedly, George left his spot in the window, flew over to the old wooden barrel and peered into the glass. He came face to face with a lady of a well-to-do stature with a furrowed brow looking extremely cross.

"What are you going to do about my missing carpet?" she continued angrily, raising both hands impatiently to emphasise the severity of the problem.

"It looks like I'm going to be staying here a bit longer, George," Gypsy said with a grin, removing her cloak and hanging it back up on the makeshift coat rack. "Are you ready for another adventure?"

George grinned with excitement before crying out with glee. "You bet!"

About the Author

After leaving behind the corporate world of working in London, Hayley Dartnell found herself in lockdown writing a short story about a little cloth doll she had made. A true believer in fairytales and all things magical, her imagination went into overdrive as she listened to her inner child speak. She divides her time between Devon and Cambridgeshire.

To see the Lavender Fairies brought to life visit their Instagram page:

www.instagram.com/lavenderfairyadventures

Also in this series:

Book 1 of *Lavender Fairy Adventures*:

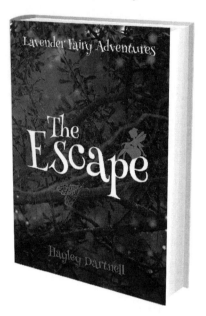

If you were a woodland creature in trouble, who would you turn to for help?

It's summertime in Bluebell Meadow and George the Moth has run away from a notorious woodland gang called the Marsh Beasts. In his haste to get away, George finds himself in danger.

Will the Lavender Fairies come to the rescue?

A magical story filled with enchantment, friendship and kindness.

Printed in Great Britain
by Amazon

67735840R00050